EASY ON THE SOUL

Folktales for Adults

David Hench

authorHOUSE®

AuthorHouse™
1663 Liberty Drive
Bloomington, IN 47403
www.authorhouse.com
Phone: 1 (800) 839-8640

This is a work of fiction. All of the characters, names, incidents,
organizations, and dialogue in this novel are either the products
of the author's imagination or are used fictitiously.

Published by AuthorHouse   07/18/2017

ISBN: 978-1-5246-9942-0 (sc)
ISBN: 978-1-5246-9940-6 (hc)
ISBN: 978-1-5246-9941-3 (e)

Library of Congress Control Number: 2017910739

Print information available on the last page.

"Some day you will be old enough to read folktales again."

– C. S. Lewis

The stories herein are hybrid "spiritual/psychological folktales."

Perhaps exactly along the lines of the sentiment above.

Join the author for these delightful folktales, which include one re-telling of a classic and eight originals-first-time-ever-in-print. The wisdom of the ages is passed down through such seemingly simple stories ... through their drama, themes and characters ... even at times helping us reassess the values we live by. So here we go ... off to times and places more charming and magical than the lands we so oft inhabit. "Open sesame," then, on the land of enchantment ...

Illustrated by:

Whitney Leigh Carpenter -- a painter/illustrator based in Louisville, Kentucky.

and by

Brian Dickson -- an artist and world resident currently located in The Villages, Florida.

By David Hench

Contents

The Days of the Sprites

Back in the time before the human race was so lost there was a breed of sprites, a kind of spirit or pixie, but wiser, that looked in on the human types and helped keep them on the right path.

"What's news in your world?" they might pop in and whisper in the ear of a troubled person, already knowing themselves really, but asking as to offer wisdom upon the matter.

One aging person lamented, "I can't do what I used to do."

The sprite said, "Maybe it's time to focus elsewhere." And he popped back out … gone as quickly as he came.

Another aging one said, "My knees are hurting and neither can I swing a golf club as in my glory days."

"That wasn't your glory," said the sprite. "That was the glorification of diversion. Life itself beckons you now. Let's not worry so much about how good you are at golf." Poof: gone.

Another unwise aging one was sitting watching television and a sprite popped in: "What's news in the world of Joe?" it said to him.

"I have not many more years to amass money and possessions as I've always done. Truth be told, materialism is my creed, but I can't take it with me."

"What can you take with you?" answered the sprite.

"I don't know," said Joe the human.

"What is immaterial that perhaps exists in other planes?" asked the sprite … leaving Joe to think.

Across the globe a sprite popped in on another unsuspecting aging one. "What's life doing with you, friend?" it asked.

"What good am I now? I am a shell of my former self," he lamented.

"The former self was a shell of you, worthy one," said the sprite. "Consider now your true self, and life, rather than your shell self and its diversions." Poof, gone.

Of her very considerable beauty, a fine woman lamented its diminishment. Poof: "What's new in your world, lovely spirit?" asked the sprite.

"I fear loss … and yes, loss of beauty," said the woman.

"Beauty is a gift: be grateful. So too it is apportioned for a time and then given to others upcoming. Is this okay with you? Beauty moves inward for the wise.

What other beauty do you have, for nothing stays the same, most fortunate one?" This was a lot to say for a sprite, but the subject required it.

As soon as they appeared they were gone, the sprites were, but always leaving a thought of sagacity behind. Their message was never in support of worldly success, youthful folly, or foolish pursuits and other such futile scorecards of life. "Let the diversions that you lose as you age help center your attention on wiser things," was central to their message.

To a hospice patient named Bev dying of pancreatic cancer, a sprite popped into being and asked, "What's your heart, cherished one?"

She said: "All is progressing. I am ready to release my attachments here, ready for the unknown. Wasn't life once unknown as well? Praise be to life and to its ways, including this last."

"You learn wisely. Soon you will be a sprite," said the wispy, tiny phantom.

After a little while the fledgling sprite popped into a hospital room. "What's life doing with you currently?" it said.

"Oh, woe is me," said the person. "I have heart trouble. Maybe the rat race is killing me."

"Maybe you could step off the hamster wheel. The rat race is likewise a futile trek. It is in vain and a chasing after the wind, worthy friend."

Instantly the fledgling sprite popped up across the world and said to a person, "What's up in your human life?"

"I am quite depressed in life," the fine lady said.

"Activity is key," said the sprite. "Depression is characterized by doing and thinking very little (except maybe worrying). Get active. Both physical and mental activity, when possible, can help enormously." This thought, planted in the lady's mind, indeed helped her predicament.

Still again, learning the ropes, it popped in on someone, saying, "Hello. How do you find yourself, fine sir?"

"Huh? Who's there? Oh, whoever you are, I have become very unhappy," bemoaned the person.

"Do you have a purpose or a project? Have you helped someone else who might be unhappy?" the ether seemed to say. Poof. Gone.

To another perfectly healthy one he popped in and said: "Hello, fellow traveler. What is your scorecard for life?"

"Huh? What? Who would ask such a question?" Poof.

To another aging one he popped in.

"For what is my decline?" he asked the sprite.

"Aging is not a curse, unless your measure of life is how well you play golf and such," answered the fledgling sprite. "In spiritual circles many speak of the wisdom of slowing down. Well, aging makes you slow down, and is a nudge toward evolution and enlightenment."

Poof the sprite was gone having accomplished its first missions of enlightenment. "I wonder where I got some of that," thought the sprite, confused … for it was unbeknownst to the rookie sprites that they received wisdom from the universe.

The sprites continued their campaign to awaken the lost human students. Consider, reader, that which a good book says: A wise person heeds worthy counsel, but a foolish one eschews it and carries on as before.

It went on and on like this with the sprites popping in giving wise offerings to the people. It was a mystery where the sprites came from, but they helped keep people on a good path. These were very magical times … until the day when the people stopped listening. For sprites do not go where they are not welcome. This began mankind's great lost era – where no one heeded wisdom and many were lost on an errant path with wayward scorecards. A sad, sad time. No magic.

Still in the ether there are whispers. Are you listening?

Mitzie the Faithful

(An ancient folktale for adults)

The Players

Mitzie	....	Protagonist and heroine
Mortuus the Terrible	....	Antagonist, Personification of Death
The King	....	Mitzie's father and the benevolent king
The Grand Queen of Kindness	....	Mitzie's mother taken by the plague
Baby twin sister	....	Mitzie's sister also claimed by the plague
Jackson the Playful	....	Mitzie's puppy

The Story

Long ago in the olden times when fairy tales were still real, there was a kingdom of good people who were terribly afraid. A great scourge had visited their kingdom and taken a tragic toll. The dreaded visitor was death. Mortuus the Terrible had invaded without mercy.

The normally joyful people were so bereaved and worried that all happiness had come to a halt. The good King was powerless to help, as his palace was struck by the scourge as well. His wife, the Grand Queen of Kindness, had succumbed, as had one of their baby twin girls. Nowhere was there ever more sadness.

Mortuus had even taken over a wing of the King's palace. No one could prevent it. All who tried, who even dared tread into the Dark Wing, never returned. The whole wing was shut off as Mortuus continued to have his way with the kingdom ... and the plague raged on.

One of the few bright spots in the kingdom was the surviving twin girl of the celebrated royal twins, who was growing in faith and strength. The good spirits from before the disaster were recalled by those watching her grow. She was smart, fun loving, caring, honest, pretty, curious ... and much more. The King had given her a title to grow into: Mitzie the Faithful.

She liked this title okay but considered it a little stuffy. So she jokingly called her beloved puppy "Jackson the Playful." They were forever running around the palace playing fetch and hide and seek. Everyone kept her away from the Dark Wing ... and she was careful to obey.

But one day Mitzie was riding her tricycle through the palace chasing Jackson, when she accidentally wheeled into the closed wing. Mortuus had left the door open slyly. She startled when there he stood towering over her. The Terrible One closed the door behind her slowly … and threw the bolt.

When she could not be found, the King and his court, and all the people were panicked … for no one had ever crossed the threshold and returned. They could not get into the Dark Wing to help.

She was gone. Mitzie the Faithful, on whose head the spirits of the kingdom rested, gone? The kingdom plunged further into despair at the tragic news.

There in the Dark Wing before Mortuus, Mitzie was frozen in terror.

"Who are you?" she mumbled to him.

"All know me, or will," was his reply.

Mitzie tried to ride by him on her trike. But he stopped her.

"I have you now," he said, ominously.

"What are you going to do with me?" Mitzie asked so innocently that the beast was a little startled by it.

He said nothing.

The beast surprised himself by choosing to keep the girl's company for a while. At first Mitzie shuddered in his presence, but gradually she began to feel something less scary coming from him ... even began to trust him a little, to trust that he wouldn't harm her.

Mortuus felt some of his own innocence, some of his own humanity as a result of this new friend. Soon, though, he went back into character of being a beast. "You are mine. You will never return to the world," he bellowed.

Thus began the fluctuating of the heart of Mortuus the Terrible. With each succeeding day, Mitzie's spirit slowly began to win him over once again.

Then the unexpected happened. With the return of his humanity also came his mortality.

Mortuus the Terrible got sick.

Mitzie now ministered to him the same way she had learned to care for her sister when she became ill.

This won the beast over and he yielded his heart of stone. As life slipped from his veins, Mitzie added love to his heart. He began to divulge his secrets to her to take back to the people of the kingdom. For suddenly, the beast wanted to help humanity, not terrorize it.

"Why did you scare everybody so and cause so much heartache and tragedy?" Mitzie asked.

"It was my lot," wept the Terrible One. "I didn't choose it."

At this the terrible beast handed Mitzie a beautifully ornate hand mirror, through which she could see the people who had passed on. When she saw her mother and sister, Mitzie's joy at seeing them again melted the beast's remaining callousness.

Again he began to divulge his secrets, this time wholeheartedly, and Mitzie, becoming a young woman now, having been captive many years, listened attentively.

Mitzie cared for him and heard his unburdening as his sickness progressed. She was free to leave now for he could no longer stop her, but when she started to she heard a voice telling her to stay. She was unsure because she didn't recognize the voice. But stay she did in the Dark Wing, and showed kindness toward the beast. No longer was he terrible. He was a dying, sensitive, worthy soul. Before his end came the curtains were drawn and the Dark Wing became light.

Upon his death two spirits appeared to help, and Mitzie held a burial ceremony.

"To dust your body returns," prayed Mitzie, "but your soul and wisdom will be kept in my heart. You will be remembered dearly." Mitzie said these words through tears over what was once a beast.

It was now time for her return to the kingdom. "A fine deed, faithful one," said the mysterious voice regarding all this. Then the door to the secluded wing opened itself, and Mitzie walked through anxiously. Her governess and soon the King – and then the whole kingdom – were amazed and rejoiced over her return. A huge celebration and banquet was held. Toasts and joyous laughter reigned. After the celebration, everyone wanted to know what had transpired in the years she was gone.

They couldn't have known on the outside what was happening ... and how Mitzie had befriended the creature. Dreaded though he was, behind his mask of death and ugliness was a wounded soul. Faithful Mitzie had awakened in him his lost humanity. As she cared for him, the two in isolation, her presumed lost ... he began to teach her about his mission for which he was so reviled. All this she now told her fellow citizens.

She had found his *Book of Passings*, she told them, which chronicled all deaths. In it was her mother and sister's names. Mitzie had cried as she innocently asked about why he took them. The Terrible One had at last felt his heart.

Becoming human again, Mortuus the Terrible, eternal soul collector and monster, was now human and mortal himself ... his curse lifted. On his deathbed, afraid himself, he taught me of death, Mitzie recounted. He had given up his reign of terror willingly and granted Mitzie to return to the kingdom.

Soon, in keeping with their tradition, the people gathered under the moonlight at an outdoor amphitheater to hear teachings. Speakers emerged as if magically from the back and below, down a secret sidewalk and up on to the stage. All was still, the air crisp and cool. Nature seemed to be paused, to be present, to be looking on. Mitzie the Faithful stood tall and strong and these were her tellings to the people:

"Blessed is mourning ... for it is a derivative of love.

Reverence for life and for death are proper.

Though it comes with trembling – because it comes with trembling – death is a touchstone …
for whomever is trembling has been made genuine.

In your depths reside clues about the great beyond.

Life and death are set before you; which do you choose?

A phobia of death hinders life. Know this adversary if it is in you.

Blessed are the good who die young. Double is the sadness of their passing.

Sadness touches your humanity; it is not an enemy.

The black clouds of bereavement are necessary, but also temporary. The sun also rises. Do not give bereavement the last word.

Celebrate your departed loved ones, don't just mourn them. What tremendously valuable life! Pay tribute to it.

Our wakings are numbered under the sun. Make peace with this.

Your body is a mortal and temporary machine. Consider this, accept this, worthy sojourner, and your steps gain wisdom.

Death after a long, full life is as natural and as welcome as sleep after a long, full day."

She paused and then continued:

What is death? Man cannot know it. It is part of the Great Mystery. It could be a portal to the next level of being.

If you still have life, you still have lessons. Use your life wisely to learn them.

With death always on the horizon, take not death as a curse but rather life as a wondrous gift.

Death is the keeper of former lives … where none are abandoned.

Fear not, worthy sojourner. Let your earthly time be a blessing to many.

I have spoken with Mortuus the Terrible. At your last, says he, will your spirit truly dance."

The people were moved by her speaking, for her message was manna to the long saddened kingdom. The days upcoming were full of hope and caring: for the young and the old, for the healthy and the sick, for the privileged and the downtrodden, for the acclaimed and the modest. For all there was renewed faith in life and less dread of death.

Mitzie the Faithful reigned for many years, becoming known as "Sister Keeper of Souls." The wing of the palace formerly haunted by the specter of death was now dedicated to all loved ones: none were abandoned or forgotten. All souls, past and present, were kept close. This was a peaceful thought for all who had loved ones departed. The pages of the calendar started turning more lightly. The days of the kingdom rejoiced. Life was to be lived with joy once again … ever mindful of those departed and mindful too that where there is yet life … it is meant to be lived. Happiness was possible once more and the music of life was rising anew … never to be silenced in a kingdom where death had become teacher to the good people.

The Queen, the Priestess, and the Maven

There once was a boy who was very anxious and shy. Sadly, when he was ten his mother became ill and passed away, and to further the tragedy, his new home was cold and ugly. He felt so uncomfortable and stressed in his new home that one day he ran off into the woods to get away. There he wandered feeling lost and alone, but he didn't want to admit, either to himself or to anyone else, how badly he felt.

Soon a falcon swooped into his path and then soared majestically above into the sky. Startled pleasantly by this, the boy decided to follow below in the bird's path.

After a while of following he came upon a grand palace out in the woods, on which the stately falcon had alighted. "Wow," he thought, "that must be a wonderful place to live."

He went up and knocked on the huge, ornamental front door. A beautiful, regal, blond-haired, blue-eyed Queen answered and greeted him very sweetly.

"My, what a nice boy my woods have brought to me today," she said, hugging the little boy. What is your name?"

"I'm Oliver," said the boy.

"Hello, Oliver. What can I do for you?" she asked.

The regal Queen seemed very maternal and benevolent so he wanted to talk to her, and even more importantly, to hear her talk to him. "I lost my home and I'm wandering in the woods," Oliver said. "Will you tell me something, please?"

"Yes."

"Where is my family?"

The wise and compassionate Queen told him that though not all little ones have loving and supportive families, there is always hope to find one in your future. Oliver could tell just by looking at her and listening to her that her words had meaning and truth, and he loved the way that felt.

He thanked her gratefully, and feeling adventurous and more spirited, continued on in his walking under the falcon's path. After a while he came upon a modestly charming home in the countryside and knocked on the door. A tall, handsome, and graceful Priestess answered the door, smiled and hugged him kindly, and welcomed him in.

This wise Priestess could see that deep-down the boy was troubled. She was a studier of the heavens, the human spirit, and the future and could see many such things.

"Where is my future?" Little Oliver asked her earnestly.

With this Priestess you couldn't miss her joyous yet thoughtful expressions, and she flashed it at him now. "You create your own future..." she began, and told him her story of recreating her own life. Oliver soaked it in, loving every minute of the story. Before she took his leave (to return to one of her favorite afternoon jigsaw puzzles), she advised him strongly not to let fear keep him from creating a good future. She gave him a hug that stirred something deep in him. This feeling felt something like a home within himself.

The Priestess' counsel about fear gave him much food for thought as he left again on his walk, because he didn't know very much about his fear at all. Through the woods he walked and thought about it. He soon heard the call of the falcon and followed it again.

In a little while he came to striking Tudor-style home at the end of a long, winding driveway lined with woods and pastures. He knocked on the door.

Now a slender, dark haired beauty called The Maven opened the door.

"Are you lost?" she asked Oliver.

"No. I'm wandering," he said.

"Oh. Okay. What can I do?" said The Maven, smiling at his apparent precociousness.

"I want to ask you a question," continued Oliver.

"I love questions," she said.

"Where is my fear?" he asked.

"That's a complicated one," said the Maven showing him in. And she sat with him.

"If you send your fear away to where you don't think about it, it remains alive," she said. "Its hidden hand then controls much of your life. But if you bring it into focus and face it head on, it loses power over you. So, do not deny your fear because you think it is uncool to be afraid or because it is troubling; it is part of you and it is okay that it is part of you. Accept it, make friends with it. For denied fear is a robber of life, and love, on the other hand, is a sprouting of wings under whose influence possibilities skyrocket."

"Skyrockets all the way up into the sky? Up with my bird friend, the falcon?" Oliver asked. "The Priestess who I just visited loves the sky and even pointed out the clouds and colors up there," he continued.

"Did she now?" said the Maven. "I know her and that sounds just like her. What a nice lady she is, don't you think?"

"Yes I do. She talked about my real self and said I would discover that it was good if I could really find it."

"She's right about that," said the Maven. "The important part is looking for it and uncovering this truth…*that the self is tasked at birth to realize its goodness.*" She put her arms around his shoulders with these gentle words, letting him feel the involvement of another consciousness influencing him to become good.

Oliver the orphan battled his resistance to let her care, to let her in. That was fear talking. A terrible, threatening thing it seemed to him to let someone touch your actual self. His life had become a pattern of sealing off from the world. The Maven seemed able to salve this problem.

With his third visit of the day complete, young Oliver walked onto the front porch of the Maven's home. There the falcon was perched on the rail looking straight at him.

"Where shall I go now?" Oliver asked his winged guide.

"Back to the self," said the knowing falcon. "The true self in you is the seed and gift of god. Do not negate your existence because you have failed to soar majestically. It is written: Man is brought low by the mighty hand of truth before he may be found worthy of being exalted. Stay with your self then regardless of its difficulties. Do not condemn and abandon it:

ever. That is a terrible mistake. For goodness lies in caring for and improving of the self and in showing compassion and aid for others in this quest."

The truth-speaking falcon was the shared pet bird of the three grand ladies of the forest. Together they came to the aid of all lost souls who traversed their woods. Children, most of all, came out of their woods on a new path. They found their fear, looked to their future with hope, and eventually nestled into a home that was full of love and support where all were cherished. And happiness for all was the wonderful end of the story in the wisdom-teaching land of The Queen, The Priestess, and The Maven.

JANSTER SEAGULL

A lovely Maven, who was a human person at the moment, toiled in her woods assiduously and faithfully. Life was difficult at times because the fruits were not always immediate or easily recognized. But her spirit was one of plentiful love and joy. One fateful day, she became Janster Seagull and was seen flying over the woods, surveying the goings on of her own life. And she saw that it was good, that it was sacred. She soared mightily and with great spirit over this realization. She flew the fancy and daring flights of her kindred gulls. It was historic, man ... righteous, bodacious, *epical*, worthy of lyrical musings. You couldn't bring her down. She wouldn't land.

And then one day darned if Janster Seagull didn't turn her beak to the sky and soar directly toward the heavens. She was going for the thrilling High Dive of gullian lore. When she finally topped out, she rolled, tucked her wings, and dove for all she was worth. Chief Seagull looked on at this spirited display of his own patented maneuver with favor, as the horses on the farm below, Nick, Double Dipper, Grey Love, and Brown Beauty watched raptly. Animals dug this kind of thing. It was the horses version of running in the wind for all they were worth. Also watching was a legendary guru of the flock, Deepak Seagull, who had been making note of the efforts of the Janster gull.

Janster Seagull's woods were a spiritual world of adventure as well as a land of trial and diligence. It was much to be worthy of such a land, but Chief Seagull and Deepak were well-pleased.

As a shape-shifted gull now, Janster Seagull felt a draw to the sea. Of course! One day she unexpectedly turned east on one of her flights, feeling its pull. She began to smell the ocean currents as she flew. Every feather on Janster Seagull stood straight up in excitement as she swooped into the ocean scene of her old gull friends. They clamored around her and there were bukoos of affectionate beak nuzzles and playful wing taps. And flock they did! Now was the time to dive toward the breakers and buzz the beachgoers playfully.

Janster Seagull was a gull of many hats. She was full of work and play, joy and pain, seriousness and silliness, steadfastness and flightiness, but most of all, she was full of love for life. Loving life for a seagull meant flying passionately, flocking together with loved ones, offering a helping hand to others, and always believing in everyone's innate goodness. That was the code she flew by.

Now Janster Seagull was cruising her airspace …
gracefully, athletically … like that rare athlete that
is poetry in motion and mesmerizes with their
gait. Her mood was still and quiet; she didn't need
constant highs to reassure her. She relied not on highs
and shallow standards for her security, but on her
gullness … which was her oneness with gull nature.
She was about flying and being, and celebrating both,
not about fake scorecards in life. One could say she
had drifted out of the main currents of cultural values
and into a different value stream. In her flights she
embodied and delivered this special message to all
animals, but especially to wounded gulls. She was
beloved by her followers; for they were legion awaiting
her message of medicine: "Your goodness and your
value are within." The thrilling excitement of it was
almost – almost – more than they could bear. They
put their heads and hearts together to try to fly in her
draft.

Janster Seagull was flying with a special gleam in her eye this day … in a mischievous mood of the kind that in her human moments she was known to walk on the furniture (which everyone knows you aren't supposed to do). In such moods, she forgot all convention, all troubles, concerns of all kinds … and LIVED. This was a good lesson she had learned and then passed on to the flock. Presence is actually the absence of a lot of undesirable things (like fear, shame, unworthiness), but animals don't have this problem, just people. Janster Seagull flew with the true Self wide open.

Shapeshifter

Flying was her love. So what did she do this day? She flew upside-down through restricted gull airspace and then buzzed the waves and the sharks without compunction! Oh man, this was one gull.

Convenings of the boss gulls were arranged to address her unruliness, where they deliberated about what sanctions to impose. It was decreed that she would remain unsanctioned while the case was referred to the venerated Deepak Seagull, whose wisdom was well-known in such cases, and who was currently vacationing on the Jersey Shore where he was flying around the boardwalk people-watching the tourists. Janster Seagull's eyes got big when she heard her case was being referred to Deepak. She knew of him and was a big fan.

(**Stay tuned for our next episode of gullian adventures. Same gull time, same gull channel.**)

Episode 2

The Honorary Deepak Seagull presiding: court in session.

Deepak Seagull was a no-nonsense judge of wide repute. He had come to court this morn expecting a bad-acting, recidivist perp, needing the book thrown at him (and maybe the key thrown away too). What he got was Janster Seagull ... a youthful, wide-eyed, alluring, good-hearted defendant if there ever was one.

At first he thought she was the new court stenographer. When she stood up and pled guilty to unruly flying, of all ridiculous things, he fell silent for several seconds, then called counsel to the bench.

Barrister Nathaniel Thunderbird – quite the lawyerly type – wanted to prosecute to the full extent of the law and deny her all flying and leadership privileges. "De-wing her," he said, "she's guilty and needs punishment."

Alice Seagull, who flew in from Switzerland to defend Janster, smelled a rat in the proceedings.

"Who would not encourage self-expression of this gull, and why?" she demanded to the court.

The prosecutor recoiled, lowering his gaze. He wasn't used to being trumped in his arguments, or to anybody seeing what he was really up to with his pontificating.

"She defaulted on the responsibilities of being a gull, she flew in the face of the decrees of our guru, encouraging others to do the same. She has made it clear she is immoral in so doing," he raved.

Alice Seagull rose gracefully. "Really?" she said. "By what standard, other than your own unenlightened, unrecognized self-condemnation, do you condemn the struggles of another gull?"

Silence from the great mouthpiece, Nathaniel Thunderbird.

Deepak Seagull looked on trying to remain objective, trying not to be smitten by the Janster Gull and her audacious "crime."

"Miss Seagull, you flew upside-down in restricted airspace against the ways of right-flying established by your forbearers? Did you have a reason?"

"Umm, umm, umm, umm," she said, clearing her throat. "It was a beautiful day and my gullian spirit moved me to do it."

"DISMISSED!" crowed Deepak Seagull, "with sanction against barrister Nathaniel Thunderbird for prosecutorial overzealousness!"

Alice Seagull put her wing around Janster, who was confused by it all but steadfast. "Do you want to fly with me and the judge today?" asked Alice. You can bet your bottom dollar Janster Seagull was ready to fly with them.

And they lived (and flew) happily ever after. In fact they were more than happy. They were free … free to express their life force unrestrained. The freedom unto joy!

CLEVER, CLEVER GRETCHEN MOST FAIR

(An ancient and venerable tale ... as

retold here in *Easy on the Soul*)

The Players

The Grand Commodore	....	Father of Gretchen
Gretchen Most Fair	....	Protagonist and heroine
Honeycup	....	Childhood friend of Gretchen
Poppi	....	Childhood friend of Gretchen
The Pernicious One	....	Devilish one who meets boy on the road
The Guard	....	Castle guard, protector of its inhabitants
The Governess	....	Caretaker of boy David
David	....	Orphan boy roaming the earth

The Story

Act 1

Back in the times when fairy tales were real there lived a Grand Commodore, much celebrated for his seagoing adventures, who had a daughter named Gretchen. Gretchen was a clever and gracious soul, and pretty too … a more winsome lass could not be found. Highly eligible merchants and noblemen came from parts near and far to ask for her hand … some less presumptuous visitors just for a word from her charming heart. But her father would have few of them. "Whoever wins my daughters hand," said the Commodore, "will be the greatest huntsman in the land. At least!"

Now in a neighboring village there was a boy from a children's home who got it in his head that he would like a word from Gretchen. The boy's governess, knowing this was impossible, could only console him.

For though he was a good-hearted lad he was a bit simple and lacking in qualities such a prospective queen might favor. (But underrate NOT, dear reader, the fine heart of our heroine, Gretchen!)

Of his caretaker's counsel the boy David thought, "I can but try." And he dressed for the journey, grabbed his trusty gun and set out for the Commodore's castle. His caretaker's words rang in his ears as he traveled. Yet he had a secret in his soul, a good secret, that no one could know. For him, even being addressed by Gretchen would be a knighting. *"Hakarat hatov"* was the idea … *admiring the good* … and perhaps being touched by it.

Along the trail young David met a tall stranger dressed all in gothic black, with hooves for feet, horns under his fancy hat, and a very slick tongue. "Where are you going, young man?" asked this stranger.

"I am off to the castle and hope to see Gretchen Most Fair; tis Gretchen Most Fair I hope to see," said the boy. The stranger scoffed at the boy, and derided him mercilessly. "Not in a million years will they receive you," said the beastly stranger. "So be it," said the boy, undaunted ... "tis Gretchen Most Fair I wish to see."

"Her father has required that only the world's greatest and noblest meet her. You have nothing to offer in your visit," ridiculed The Beast. "But I'll tell you what I'll do, such a kind soul as I am. If you sign this paper, I can make you the world's best and noblest huntsman *presto*."

"Really? What paper? said the unsophisticated boy.

"It says that in seven years time you will go away with me and do my bidding ... unless you can stump me with a question," said The Beast.

"I think I shall, I think I might," said the boy, taken by the deal ... for seven years seemed a long time and this did seem very helpful. He signed the agreement. The Beast then took his gun and entranced it to shoot bullseyes, and departed.

David continued on to the castle. T'was Gretchen Most Fair he was off to see.

After much hiking he reached the castle grounds.

"What do you want?" the guard at the gate asked brusquely.

"I would pay my respects to Gretchen, should you favor," said David

"Ha! Good luck," snapped the guard … "leave here at once lest you be sentenced to 40 years in the dungeon, at least!" David merely sat outside the gate on a hillside, and ate his sack lunch of peanut butter and banana sandwich, undeterred.

[Interjection # 1: You don't hear about stories like this just every day. For Gretchen was in the castle playing with her friend and aspiring princess, Honeycup, and a new friend, a wild child named Poppi. But she most certainly was not allowed unannounced visitors. Gretchen at times adopted the new wild girl's hairstyle to fine effect. It looked like this when she did:

David Hench

After she had been playing with these friends for a while, Honeycup and Poppi, Gretchen Most Fair perchance glanced out her window, across the way ... and there sat the boy. If you could be hapless and content, this boy was it. When she heard why he had come, she commanded the guard to let him enter the outer gate. (Though young, Gretchen's words carried weight in the kingdom already.)

When the Grand Commodore caught wind of this and came out to inspect the boy, he laughed heartily. "So, the greatest, most noble huntsman you are, eh?" he said.

"Indeed, fine sir, but that's not why I'm here," said the boy David.

The Commodore thought this over for an instant and said, "So, could you shoot a feather off that buzzard circling the woods over nigh?"

"I can but try," said David, and he raised his trusty gun. Bang! and down fell a feather from a-high.

"Well done!" cried sympathetic, good-hearted Gretchen, watching from out her window.

"Yes" said the Commodore. But he did not care to present his prized daughter of all the land so easily.

"Could you shoot the wing off that bumblebee there buzzing across the meadow? the Commodore challenged.

"I can but try," was the reply.

Bang! and off went the wing as precisely as if sheared.

"Well done!" cried Gretchen again, all decked out in her pony tails. (It wasn't a formal day as she was expecting no visitors.)

"Yes, good aim," her father conceded, frowning now. For the boy was a shot! "But could you shoot the lance out of the hand of my shepherd over nigh across the hill, several fields over, where they are working?" (having spotted him only through his binoculars).

"Father, no huntsman living could shoot so well. Shame on you!" cried Gretchen. (See, on top of all her other fine qualities, Gretchen was fair-minded as well.)

"Let him try if he is a great huntsman!" demanded Clever Gretchen's father, the Grandest Commodore of them all.

Bang!! went the boy's gun and the shepherd's stick was splintered in all directions.

"Hooray!" yelled Gretchen Most Fair … for she had taken the boy's side over his tough treatment and obviously respectful pilgrimage. She could tell this easy, which was part of being clever … which was no problem for this Gretchen … which was lucky for the boy shooter.

Seeing all this and that he was beaten by the boy's deadly shooting, the Commodore escorted the boy into the castle proper to grant him his wish … a brief word from Gretchen.

Act II

In all lore, which the boy had read widely, a knighting was a matter of the spirit. At the first direct word from Gretchen, the unknown boy went to a knee in respect and humility. *"Hakarat hatov,"* he muttered with his eyes downcast … and he never looked up during what he considered a ceremony, but to everybody else was just a greeting.

The Commodore noticed this gesture, but limited the encounter, and directly the aspiring noble huntsman was back on the road … but with magic in his soul. Even his caretaker could not have foreseen this for him. In the years hence, it was later said, the world's fair of visitors did traipse to Gretchen's door. None were coming from quite the same place as this boy.

[Intermission]

(the curtain opens on Act III)

After seven years David, now becoming a man, once more sought the counsel of Gretchen, now a Countess, concerning the looming seven year deal with the stranger that his original trip had cost him. Seeing his predicament Gretchen's good morals told her to help.

"The Evil One tricked you," declared the more cosmopolitan Gretchen. "I'll remedy this. A question he can't answer. Hmm," she said, and began to think. (Remember, dear reader, there are two "clevers" in our title. Ha!)

At this second meeting an idea struck David. Seeing Gretchen again and hearing her plan as she now outlined it, he coined a new word that spread around the fine kingdom. The new word was: "Gretchonian." All in the kingdom agreed it was a great word and loved it for being after their favored lass. But the only problem was that nothing cool enough ever happened to use it. So everyone was stumped.

Meanwhile, get this: seeking not her father the Commodore's advice nor the assistance of her considerable brigade of guards, of her own cleverness Gretchen devised a plan to defeat the Pernicious One!

[Interjection #2: I mean, how cool is Gretchen Most Fair? This guy was a million-to-one to have ever gotten in the castle the first time years ago, and now he's back and receiving a kindness from you know who? Inconceivable! Okay, on with the story. Important, though, that no one missed this point about our heroine. Just unbelievable!]

Next morning, as the story goes, excuse me, Gretchen took off all her clothes (in her private chambers) and smeared her skin all over with syrup. Then she cut open her pillows and covered herself from head to toe with feathers.

Then she hid out. What in the world was she up to?

Presently the Evil One came to the castle, and into the lair of Gretchen Most Fair and the former boy-not-so-wonder.

"Bring me David," he demanded of the guard at the gate, "My sources tell me he seeks refuge from me here. I'll not be foiled and will bring pestilence upon this castle if you resist."

That sounded serious. *You don't bluff with pestilences ... he must have some,* thought the dense guard. Fearing the man, and for his job security probably, the guard quickly complied.

"Seven years are up today. Are you ready, David?" said the Devil through an ugly, leering smile. For he never missed such a date.

"Do I look ready?" said David. "For I am armed well for the situation. Say, shall I have one last shot for old time's sake?" he said craftily (Gretchen had crafted this.)

"Why not?" said the Evil One, and they set off together over the field.

By and by a crow flew over. "Shoot off its beak," commanded the Evil One.

"Too easy," said David.

They went a little further and a jackrabbit scampered by. "Shoot off its tail," he said.

"Child's play, and I am no longer a child," was the reply.

"Very well. I believe it is so," said the Devil.

They walked on and several fields over and across a flowered meadow was something skipping and running like a great bird, some five-and-a-half feet tall. But who ever heard of a such a bird, and skipping around? Nobody.

(It was Gretchen, with syrup and feathers from head to toe.)

"Shoot that!" the Devil yelled.

"I might," said the noble huntsman, "If only I knew what it was."

"Just shoot," was the terse reply.

"Perhaps," said the huntsman, raising his gun as if to take aim. "But what in the world is it? It's quite a sight to behold, is it not?"

"Don't worry what it is, just shoot," The Devil said.

"I never shoot at what I cannot identify," said the great huntsman. "What is it? Some kind of crazy pretty bird?"

"Oh, my agony, *I do not know!*" was the angry reply.

"Then be gone from here, for you could not answer the question that my goodhearted feathery friend, Gretchen, crafted for me. Be gone from this kingdom, Pernicious One!"

Clever Gretchen had outsmarted, bamboozled, flummoxed, discombobulated, perplexed, befuddled, outmaneuvered, and bewildered the Pernicious One! At least! ... Whereupon he fled in terror and was not heard from in the land ever again.

All was well in the kingdom. A side note: years later the finances of the kingdom fell into disarray, and Gretchen, having studied such matters, came up with an ingenious solution … saving the kingdom. "A Gretchonian Rescue" proclaimed the headlines, and the good people cheered all across the land.

After these very famous deeds, The Grand Commodore, Gretchen herself, and particularly the orphan boy wandering the earth … each were visited with many blessings in their lives. Long after she had expatriated to exotic foreign lands, and long after her celebrated return, and long after that, right up to today, the people of the kingdom told and retold many such stories about the goodness of their beloved Gretchen Most Fair …

The End.

This retelling of the tale is based in part on Alison Lurie's version, "Clever Gretchen," from her book, Clever Gretchen and Other Forgotten Folktales … and also various ancient "Skillful Huntsman" themes.

Clever Gretchen and the Three Riddles

Once upon a time there was a man and wife, and their young daughter, who were peasants living in the country. They were very poor and had precious little, but they did have what mattered most. The father loved his girl, Gretchen, more than all the world, as did his wife. It was unconditional love but Gretchen also earned it every bit. Kind, honest, thoughtful, and becoming surprisingly pretty for the tomboy she once was … she returned their love fully.

They were poor because the father was injured and blinded defending their land in a war he had helped win for their good king. Women were not allowed to work in these old days, so there was no income for the family. Times were hard, but happy they were. "Better is a little with love than a banquet and hatred served with it" goes the wise saying … and this was their lot.

Now the father had been a teacher and these days he plied his trade on but one very willing student: his prized daughter Gretchen. There were no schools in these parts, but her father made her education first priority, above all else … and he regaled her with stories about her great future life. She was not learning limitation, but opportunity and abundance.

The Bad Guy King

There came a day when Gretchen's father was in trouble with a new, greedy king for being unable to pay any tributes. Called before the king he had to plead guilty to the charge, and was sent away. Gretchen and her mother were left alone. Such a situation usually resulted in the child being sent to an orphanage and the mother being thrown out on the street.

Instead they made do and Gretchen's mother took over the teaching. This was also illegal for women to do back in these days. But necessity is the mother of invention, and Gretchen's mother had just invented the woman teacher. Gretchen doubled her efforts in study to try to help somehow and to make her father proud.

After a year her father came before the court again. Gretchen was there and hugged him tightly, trying to offer him hope. Though children were allowed, women were not so her mother had to stay home. Since he still couldn't pay he was sent off for another year.

Now this nasty king had a court jester who was a riddler. He liked to lord his cleverness over the downtrodden. After the sentencing, he offered a riddle that if solved would reduce one week from the sentence, A very cruel gesture. Here's his riddle.

> *As a whole I am balanced. Behead me and I am set nightly. Behead me again and I am the partner of "ready." Restored fully again, I am a domicile. What am I?*

The Bad King and his "court"

When the king heard this riddle he had no idea the answer. Looking at the underprivileged girl, Gretchen, he sneered and said: "Answer that one, lass, and I will marry you, and all your troubles will be over."

Clever Gretchen figured the answer. "You are a stable," she said to the jester.

The people in attendance gasped. The jester and the king were shocked beyond speech. The king soon started double-talking but he couldn't go back on his offer in front of all the people. He scheduled a session for the next day, upon which he said to Gretchen: "I will keep my word. You will become my 12th wife one week from today. All your troubles are over."

"No thank you," Gretchen said, and left the court. And all were amazed that she would turn down the king. What in the world was she up to?

Another year passed and Gretchen had gained even more in her studies and her cleverness was growing legendary. Again her much beleaguered father was before the court. Another offer of freedom was made if he could pay triple the amount due last year, but he was unable. Since women were not allowed to work for pay in those days, Gretchen or her mother could not pay it for him, though surely they would if allowed.

The jester, recognizing her from the year before, went deep into his book of riddles, hoping to taunt her. The people in the court hated this, but once again felt powerless to stop it.

Here's what he said:

> *I am greater than god and more evil than the devil? The destitute have have me yet the rich need me. If you eat me you lose weight. What am I?*

Gretchen solved the riddle in her head before he was even done. The king, drunk and stupid, didn't remember Gretchen from the year before.

"I'll tell you, sweetie," he said disgustingly, "if you answer it I will marry you and all your problems will be solved, I'll release your father, and you'll have it made with me in the palace as one of my many happy wives."

Gretchen gave her answer, surprising the jester once again. "Nothing," she said. And to the marriage proposal she said: "No thank you. I'd rather be a peasant."

The people in the court wanted to applaud but were too frightened. Once again Gretchen's admirable father was sent away (since she had rejected the deal) and the drunken king staggered off. Gretchen returned home and told her mother all, of which her mother was very proud but didn't brag. The banned teaching and studying resumed between the two.

Clever Gretchen Strikes Back

After another year the third and final hearing was held. If her father couldn't pay he would get a life sentence. Gretchen's admirable father had no form of payment. The people were appalled at the scene and a murmur was heard among them. When the ugly jester refused his usual taunt after the guilty verdict, Gretchen stood and challenged him with a riddle. The crowd was aghast. No one had ever been so defiant of royalty.

I am Copernican, American, just one time around …

And a most fateful day when freedom is found!

The jester said nothing. The king looked confused.

"Revolution!" cried Gretchen. The people revolted then and there, put the king and his court in the dungeon, and made Gretchen the new king on the spot. "Long live Clever Gretchen the First!" they cheered in unison.

The Women's Movement and Happily Ever After

Clever Gretchen was a wise and learned ruler for many years. In her footsteps came a wave of heroines bursting forth upon the lands. Cleopatra, Joan of Arc, Elizabeth I, Sappho, Catherine de Medici, Catherine the Great, Theodora of Constantinople, Mary Wollstonecraft, Eleanor of Aquitane, Theresa Avila, Jane Austen, Clara Barton, Susan B. Anthony, Helen Keller, Amelia Earhart, Benazir Bhutto, Jane Goodall, Peace Pilgrim, Eleanor Roosevelt, Marie Curie, Indira Gandhi, Rosa Parks, Margaret Thatcher, Emeline Pankhurst, Coco Chanel, Sojourner Truth, Carolyn Miles, Maya Angelou … and many, many more entered the world stage as heroines through the newly opened door.

Revolutionary minded Gretchen Most Fair, as Clever Gretchen the First, got the whole ball rolling. Of course she was very modest about her role in all this, occasionally taking a bow but mostly giving credit elsewhere … and rightfully so. For each person, man and woman, is the potential hero of their own story and it was the revolution started by Clever Gretchen that granted that possibility to the female ranks. She showed that king and his jester – showed them good – and to this day Clever Gretchen Day is celebrated in the royal and ancient kingdom.

The end.

ELEANOR TWIST

Ladies and gentlemen, honorable attendees, esteemed readers, etc. … in a long line of stately Eleanors – Eleanor of Acquitaine, Eleanor de Medici, Eleanor Roosevelt – I give you "Eleanor Twist." You're gonna like her.

I've always loved the name "Twist" myself, big time, and boy do I have a hold of a character here. Think Oliver Twist, Kid Twist … only better. Eleanor Twist, big sister and forerunner of Clever Gretchen no less, cut a mean path through folklore and I'm here to tell you about it.

Up first is her remarkable and very touching diving career, from whence she takes her distinctive moniker. Her signature dive was a front 1 ½ flip with 27 twists. Degree of difficulty: 12,000. She nailed it so many times her parents had to build a new wing on their house for all her trophies. She taught Olympian Craig Googanis everything he knows.

She was a good student, good at tennis, good at golf, a good Samaritan, a good sport, yada yada yada. I'm just covering some of the basics. She had a good laugh. Scratch that … a great laugh. Classy, stylish, elegant, she wore her blond hair short and crisp. She was cerebral, soulful. Etc.

Don't worry, like her sister she was easy on the eyes, double easy, as in deadly pretty. As in there were actually duels over her at her high school. Guys were serious about getting hitched with her in their future, and didn't cotton to anyone being overly friendly or carrying her books around for her too much. Else a shootout.

Everybody survived and when the gun smoke cleared she was at Fanderbunk University, and it was upon her fabulous matriculation there that the legend of the sisters really took off. I'll summarize: She had a 4.0 GPA, won homecoming queen, was voted most likely to succeed, got Student of the Year, and was proposed to by half the student body. The proposal thing was so out of hand she had to have a stamp made up that said "No thanks," there were so many coming in. She stamped it on the back of their hand if she liked the way they asked, and right on their forehead if she didn't. That's what Eleanor Twist did.

On the subject of courting, the same pops that later was directing traffic around Clever Gretchen was calling the shots for visitation privileges with Eleanor. In fact since she was first, he was even more impossible.

"Whoever marries my eldest daughter," said he, "will be apple of her mother's eye, the apple of Eleanor's eye, and the world's greatest this or that (whatever he thought of that day)." His normal spiel. This dad was some kind of tough case when it came to his daughters, and no one could blame him.

But Eleanor had adventure more on her mind than marrying. One day she dreamed up what adventure she wanted to become known for.

"Dearest mother," she said, "all the adventurers seem to be men and I've got it in my head to put an end to that."

Though it worried her, Eleanor's mother could hardly protest. For she had told her many times that life and the world was wide open to her.

Eleanor's plan, of all things, was to trek to the North Pole with her beloved husky, Kisha, in the lead of a team. Mother and daughter immediately began plotting how they were going to get this dangerous idea by her dad.

Meanwhile Eleanor prepared for the trek. Fate intervened when an outbreak of disease occurred in the children of the Yukon and Alaska, and they had to have medicine. Horses couldn't get there; Henry Ford and cars was way in the future; it was a dog sled or nothing. Eleanor Twist was just the gal for the job and deliver the medicine she did … in the nick of time to stem the epidemic. There were three blizzards, two avalanches, two ice flows, and an arctic cyclone …

through it all they mushed on. Eleanor had one helper,

a Sherpa, and nine dogs total, and she gave them all

equal credit to herself.

The Heroine Musher

A big deal was made about it in the *Royal and Ancient Times,* pictures and all, but Eleanor shrugged it off. She said things like: "I'm just a gal living my life and helping where I can. I really don't know what all those shootouts back in high school were about. I'm glad they all had bad aim and nobody got hurt."

I said you were gonna like her.

When Eleanor returned successfully from the North there was a big gala, with banquet, black tie and dance. Guess what her favorite dance was? Right: the twist. She was a bad mama jamma doing that twist no one could deny. And if they did they had her father to deal with, and nobody wanted that. She could twist like no other that's a fact! They'd put on some Chubby Checker sounding stuff and Eleanor took over the floor. You had to be there on that one.

They also had a crooner like Elvis Presley back then and he belted this one out: *"L'il sister can you do what your big sister does?"* After such a scintillating matriculation and adventures as Eleanor had, the odds seemed way against l'il sis measuring up. Don't worry: Gretchen got game. I'll summarize: She had 4.0, won homecoming queen, was voted most likely to succeed, got Student of the Year, was proposed to by half the student body *and by the President of the University*! (That wasn't a scandal because the president was just a kid himself having been granted the job on an interim basis when the full-time president took a sabbatical to … I forget where he went but you get the idea.) Anyway, after this sister act passed through, Fanderbunk U was never the same, I'll tell you that much.

Oh, did I mention there were "very greatest this" and "greatest that" celebrities at the gala? One was the world's greatest tycoon name of Aristotle Rockerfella. One was greatest adventurer/entrepreneur: Sir Richard Handsome. And the great one himself was there: Wayne Gretzky. Eleanor took note but kept her head.

Now she did have her eye on one lucky fella at the gala that night. Later when he popped the question to Eleanor, he said it like this: "I want to spend my days on earth with someone like you, Eleanor. One thing I do like about myself is my taste. Where's your stamp?"

Cha-ching! He received no stamp. They had a brigade of little ones so blond and bright you had to wear sunglasses to visit their home. Which was over in Chi-town where she was in charge of skyscrapers and tunnels; which was usually a man's job back then, but this Eleanor wasn't beyond "twisting" a few arms in the name of progress; which is the only way to make progress sometimes and no problem for Eleanor you-know-who; which is exactly what she did. Shew ... that was a hard sentence but I'm glad I pulled it off.

David Hench

In the pantheon of folklore heroines this one is way, way up there. And that went all the way up the line. The girls' father got "Toughest Dad" award by unanimous vote. Their mother got the award for "Bringing the Most beauty into the World." Eleanor Twist herself went down in history right next to her sister Clever Gretchen, side by side. After all, if one smart and lovely sister is glorious, two is legend. I thought it needed telling proper. At your service. The end.

Allyn Who Learned Her Truth

Long ago and far away there was a wonderful little girl who was very sensitive. Partly because of her sensitivity in a very insensitive world, she began to get bad ideas about herself.

Little Allyn also had elite intelligence and perceptiveness, and in a sometimes cruel twist of human nature, those attributes combined with sensitivity can and do conspire against a child ... a child who because of their insightfulness is picking up on things that she can't possibly handle emotionally. One of the "solutions" to this dilemma, in the child's mind, is to take horrible blames on herself. And then inevitably one must run desperately from such a negative evaluation of self, so the motor is in place to drive a profound self-alienation. "I'm really, really bad and defective, there is no way I can live integrated with this kind of self-concept, so I abandon myself and live from some alternate place."

In spite of this very human but great difficulty, Allyn matriculated to Fanderbunk University as well (see previous several stories), and quite a matriculation it was. She was valedictorian, she set the record for most time in the library, she set the record for most time up on the roof of her dorm singing the school song, she kept to herself mostly but was winsome and intriguing to all, and she used her matriculation as a springboard to a great international education.

There were many ups and downs in her youth as the battle raged in her psyche. But this story isn't about that; that's already been covered.

We fast-forward decades into the future. In these later years, Allyn reassessed her earlier troubles with self-worth and self-compassion, and learned life's greatest lesson: that valuing oneself and one's life, and that of others, is the way of wisdom.

By this time she had a multitude of advanced degrees, but this lesson was biding its time in her life. She learned something about it from a sprite (which means from the universe). It happened like this:

An exceedingly wise sprite sent specifically for this task popped in on Allyn.

"Allyn?" it said.

"Yes."

"I am visiting you from the forces of good and truth."

Allyn stayed thoughtfully quiet for a moment. After many negative visitations, something about this felt right and true.

"Okay, I think I trust that." she said.

"I'm wondering about your life, your birth, your evolution," continued the sprite ... "what are you learning about that?"

(She was a great learner, but it didn't come as readily when the focus was within. And having once been overtaken by a tsunami of negativity, Allyn had been tasked to learn a very difficult and elusive lesson about herself.)

"The ideas I was receiving were very powerful and they seemed to unseat me as originator of my thoughts," she said.

"What is good about you, Allyn?" countered the sprite.

"Well, I was given life seemingly for some good reason; I mean well in life; my true self is good and valuable and I affirm that; I work for the wellbeing of human beings whom I respect and care about; the invasion of Great Unworthiness was WRONG! Invasions don't bring truth ... the true self is not an invasion but is sometimes a casualty in life … it is the pearl within of which Rumi writes."

Allyn wasn't given to soliloquys about herself, but she was processing some of this verbally.

"Have you fed the good wolf any in your life, Allyn?" asked the sprite.

Pause. "Yes. Yes, I think I have. Education is good wolf stuff, so is character, empathy, helpfulness, constructiveness."

A truth was settling over one of the worlds sojourners. She fell silent. Deep truth needs no utterance.

A smile creeps over Allyn's face as the

good sprite broadcasts to her.

"You're the good wolf, aren't you, Allyn?" whispered the sprite.

Many years of confusion and battle were clearing and healing. In the face of any and all, the good wolf persists ... who feeds it becomes it. When we realize that the back and forth between the two wolves – even between delusional unworthiness and self-value – does not make us defective but makes us human, then the forces of dark lose power and light is in ascendancy.

Fear (the same fear as in phobias) is operating behind the dark, foreign unworthiness ... but light comes in the form of love. There is none unworthy of unconditional love and value; for such is the groundwork of goodness.

The extreme nature of some states and beliefs is a metric of sensitivity and caring – NOT of anything objective or true about the belief. So, they, such extreme states, come about from goodness ... from sensitivity and caring. That's not gymnastics. If we can come home to ourselves, extreme, alien stuff recedes.

No one really knows anything about subjects like these. But we can progress, can evolve – in our viewpoints and our experience. We can see falsehoods, uncover truths …. see with new eyes. The greatest journey – indeed – is new eyes with which to see.

Something about Allyn's struggle seemed to make her less pretentious than most, almost totally unpretentious. Telling her truth and walking her truth looked very sacred to students of it all … and to them it was highly inspiring. It helped a new path click for them – by osmosis, by identifying with it, by clarity.

Allyn Who Learned Her Truth became an archetype of mankind and womankind. It was Jungian, Laingian, human, dramatic, evolutionary, maybe revolutionary. Humanity moves toward understanding the universe and itself: that's the human story. What better representative of that is there than the person moving toward their truth? "Know thyself," counseled an ancient wise traveler … and he or she who takes up that challenge and moves toward it, instead of away from it, walks the sacred walk. The wrong ideas are left behind … and new ones welcome. Blessed are sojourners such as these – for theirs is the hero's journey.

The Tree of Contentment

Once upon a time in a parallel universe there were three young princesses-in-waiting. Two of these sisters always had big birthday bashes and were given lavish gifts. But Gretchen the stepchild, transported from another kingdom, was never treated to such. That was okay with her as she favored spiritual gifts anyway. I mean later when a girl grows up she has to have clothes and shoes, and she can't be jewel-less of course, but little significant spiritual gifts tickled Gretchen just as much as all that. Always did.

Knowing this about Gretchen was a special visitor who appeared on her 11ᵗʰ birthday. She had been riding her favorite mare, called Windhorse, and afterward was dutifully cleaning her stall as she always did. There in the stall of all things helping her was a mini-man type imp, if you can believe it. Unbeknownst to Gretchen he brought tidings from the great beyond. Gretchen adored him and treated him so kindly that, before he left, he offered her the tiniest of gifts. It was but a single seed in a little package, which he implored her to plant in her yard. Appreciative of the kind gesture, she did just that.

There in the stall of all thing helping her was a

mini-man type imp, if you can believe it.

When she rode by the people grinned ...

When Gretchen woke up the next morning, the tree had grown magically overnight to 10 feet tall. Impossibly, it bore many different kinds of fruit on its branches … apples, pineapples, kiwi, pears, plums, grapes (that would come in extra handy later in life), melons, apricots, avocados, lemons, berries, etc. All, she came to learn, would be beautifully ripe at all times … and all were golden colored. When eaten they magically supplied health, happiness, beauty, fortune and all things good – as long, that is, as Gretchen herself plucked it. She benefited greatly from the blessed fruit and gave it generously to those close to her. "All this from a such a little, cute guy?" she thought. "Hmm."

Gretchen blasted through a glorious youth, she did, which was happy and fulfilling and so much more. All was well with her life.

But there is a time for being glorious and a time for humble learning. Gretchen 1.0 is something, but wisdom is another step beyond even legendary beauty and cleverness. It is never given to 1.0 versions … not even to Gretchen. Gretchen learned this truth and conscientiously set herself toward this new task, as she always did in life. Her heart was right, her soul open.

It was in these later days that a Grand Mystic appeared to Gretchen. He appeared not to Clever Gretchen or to Gretchen Most Fair, but to Gretchen. There are roles and incarnations in life … then there is ultimate Self. The friendly mystic had no wisdom, no answers … only a compliment for how she had treated his emissary imp years ago. And he spoke to this ultimate self I mentioned, as a nudge toward her 2.0 incarnation.

"I saw a picture of you at a New Year's Eve party, if I may," said the mystic … "your priceless expression seemed to say, 'I am very happy in life and in this incarnation of myself, but there is yet more, I think."

Gretchen thought back. "Yes I remember. I seemed to get quite a few compliments on that photo," she said modestly. "Quite a feeling I had there. I was feeling very pleased and contented, and grateful, and also in that moment that maybe there was something more in store for me."

This something more was not in the way of materialism or earthly goods or this and that, but in the way of incorporeal things, otherworldly things. To whom much is given it is easy to lose one's way. Or, as a good book says, it is easier for a rope to pass through the eye of a needle than for the fortunate to appreciate this other domain.

But Gretchen was not foolish in this respect or in any other. Indeed it is true that wisdom is never given freely, but openness toward it is the requisite attitude for the shift into 2.0 versions

This was to be a new avenue of endeavor for Gretchen. Wisdom, after all, is in length of days and length of days only … it does not visit youth. So, we stay open, stay unwed to material things though appreciating them … and see where our later years lead us.

What does a Clever Gretchen 2.0 look like? What do you do for an encore when you've been a king, a heroine, a favored lass of multiple kingdoms, and the fountainhead of feminism? Don't ask me, I'm just the narrator. Nobody knows what their next version will be, anyway. But, dear reader, our 2.0 version is better than the 1.0 except in the perception of an upside-down culture, be assured.

Gretchen had been so busy in youth she had slipped slightly in her appreciation of her magical tree and what it might mean. Realizing this now, she went out and sat under it and stayed still, letting her self catch up to the moment, letting her being catch up to her doing. She scheduled 30 minutes per day – from 4:00 till 4:30 – for sitting under the tree calmly and idly. Just waiting, just being. Not as Clever Gretchen, or the beauty queen, or King Gretchen the First ... just as a student of life. It was a welcoming of her 2.0 self – whatever that might be.

"Life? Hmmm," she thought, under her magical tree. "I did that, I did that," she thought ... mentally checking things off her must-do list. Cleverness was always helpful in figuring things out for her but intuition and the heart saw more clearly here. "Everything is fine," she continued thinking, "but this spirit is visiting me. And this tree that has always blessed me. Hmm. What was that all about anyway?"

David Hench

Quite An Enchanted Tree

Clever, Clever Gretchen Most Fair was moving toward a new incarnation of herself. Exceedingly handsome? Not so important here. Exceedingly clever? Same thing, not so important here. What is important, sayeth the universe, is the 2.0 self.

Life is to be lived fully and unreservedly in youth. But "the unexamined life is not worth living," someone famous once said, and it is in this task that our ultimate value is realized. An imp and a mystic, humble sojourners themselves, appeared to Gretchen concerning this. They offered no wisdom, no answers.

They brought respect and appreciation. This "hakarot hatov" thing has versions, you folklore heroine you. The universe applauds 1.0 versions enthusiastically, of course … but it awaits 2.0s with a very keen interest. This is an issue that arises for all. For it is in the pages of our 2.0 versions that the universe quickens a new mission, which promises to be our coolest story of all …

Printed in the United States
By Bookmasters